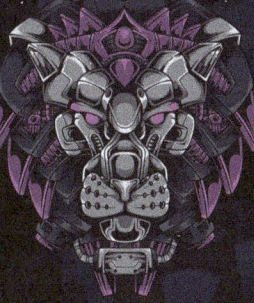

SENS!'IL STUDIOS

AARU EN DUAT

READ TODAY

OFFICIAL WEBSITE

WELCOME TO THE FUTURE

IN THE YEAR 140 OF THE 3RD ERA, THE **PLANET ALKEBULAN UNITY ALLIANCE** LAUNCHED A SPACE COLONIZATION PROJECT. THE PRIMARY PURPOSE OF THE **KUPAA INITIATIVE** IS TO ESTABLISH HUMAN SETTLEMENTS ON DISTANT PLANETS, BUT THE SEVENTH FLEET IS UNIQUE.

DECADES PRIOR A TRANSMISSION WAS DISCOVERED THAT ORIGINATED FROM THE **LIZA NYOTA** STAR SYSTEM. IT IS THE FIRST CONTACT FROM EXTRATERRESTRIAL LIFE IN MODERN HISTORY.

AFTER 2 YEARS OF FASTER THAN LIGHT TRAVEL, KUPAA FLEET 7 APPROACHES THE TARGET PLANET, **PANTHERA**, WHERE THE HIGH HOPES OF THE CREW ARE QUICKLY TRANSMUTED INTO ADRENALINE...

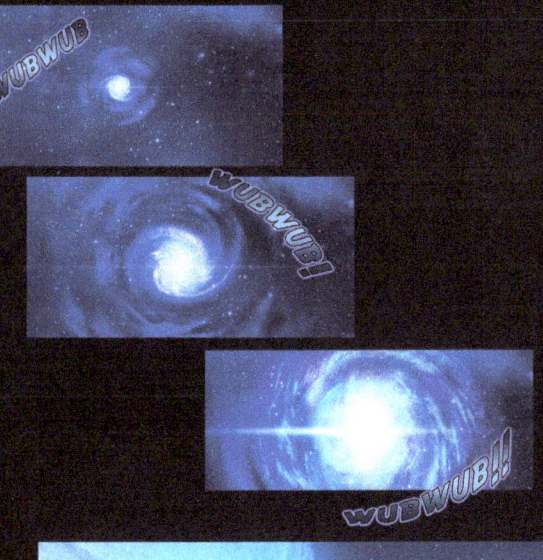

MWM WMW

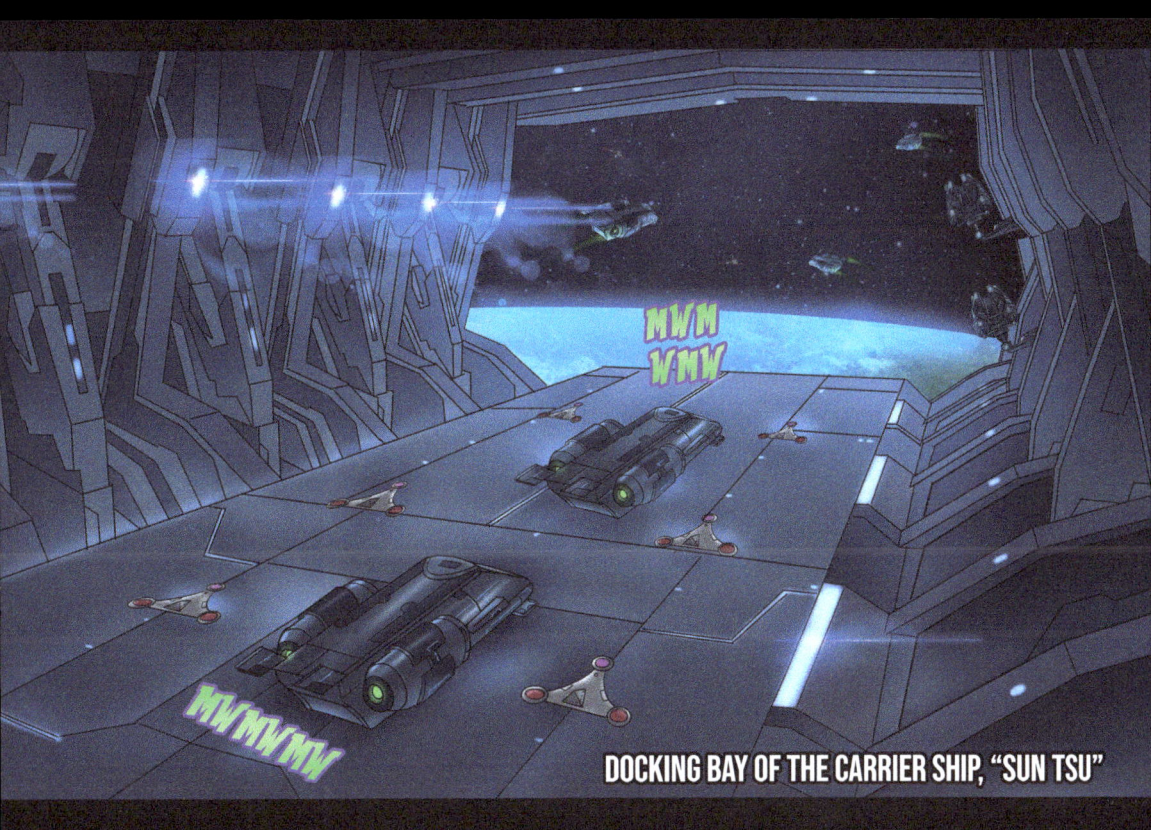

MWMWMW

DOCKING BAY OF THE CARRIER SHIP, "SUN TSU"

COMMANDER OF SPECIAL TACTICS FORCE 7

SEVEN

"COMPENSATE FOR THE ENERGY WAVES FROM THE WARP GATE. I BARELY WANT TO FEEL THE SHIP HUMMING WHEN WE BREAK ATMO."

TAP

BEEP

BEEP

MEANWHILE...

"BRING HER DOWN GENTLY OVER THERE. THAT'S THE SETTLEMENT SITE."

MWMWMWMW

WOOSH!!

WHRR!!

WHRR!!

SCAN

SEVEN HAS ALWAYS HAD A HARD TIME INVOKING HER AUTHORITY WITH ORGANIC COUNTERPARTS. PART OF HER CORE PROGRAMMING FROM DR. MGANI MADE HER THAT WAY TO KEEP HER FROM GOING ROGUE AND WHILE IT HAD ITS USES IN HER INFANCY, IT'S BECOMING A PROBLEM. SEVEN REVERED MGANI AS A MOTHER AND EVEN THOUGH SHE PASSED AWAY, SEVEN STILL HAD THE URGE TO LIVE UP TO HER EXPECTATIONS AND DESIGN. OUT OF RESPECT.

THE HIKE TO THE MOUNTAIN WAS CALMING.

THE BINARY MOONS MUT AND AMUNET GUIDED KANJI ACROSS THE FOREIGN LAND.

BUT WHEN KANJI SQUAD GOT TO THE DARK FOREST, THE ATMOSPHERE CHANGED...

THE TEAM WAS ON EDGE AS WHISPERS CALLED FROM THE DARKNESS.

SMART LENSE

THE CANOPY BLOTTED OUT ANY MOONLIGHT WHICH MADE THEM DEPENDENT ON THEIR SMART LENSE NIGHT VISION. IN THE DISTANCE, SHAPES SHIFTED AND SMUDGES OF BLACKNESS MOVED ACROSS THE DARKENED LANDSCAPE.

CREATURES OF THE NIGHT HISSED AND MOANED AS THE THREE INTERLOPERS INTRUDED ON THE ECOSYSTEM.

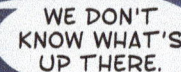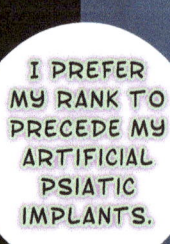

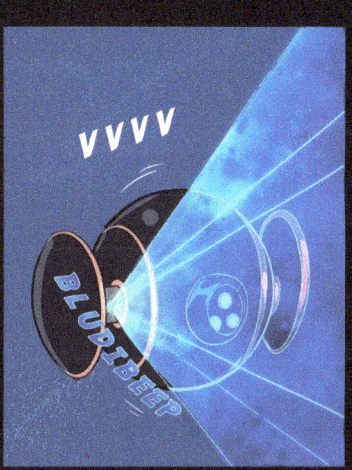

Seven didn't know what the creatures were that she was seeing in the area around Kanji, but they were bringing up all kinds of weird readings when the overhead drone scanned them.

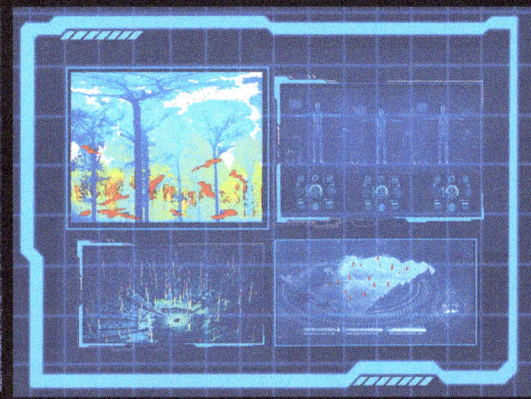

"DIDN'T KNOW YOU WERE AN A-P. GOOD THING WE CAME PREPARED WITH THESE WALL CRAWLERS."

A-P

WEAK

NOT A "REAL" PSIATIC WARRIOR

ARTIFICIAL

FAKE

"IF YOU TWO WERE REALLY AS STRONG AS YOUR FILE SAYS, YOU SHOULD HAVE BEEN ABLE TO DO THIS NATURALLY."

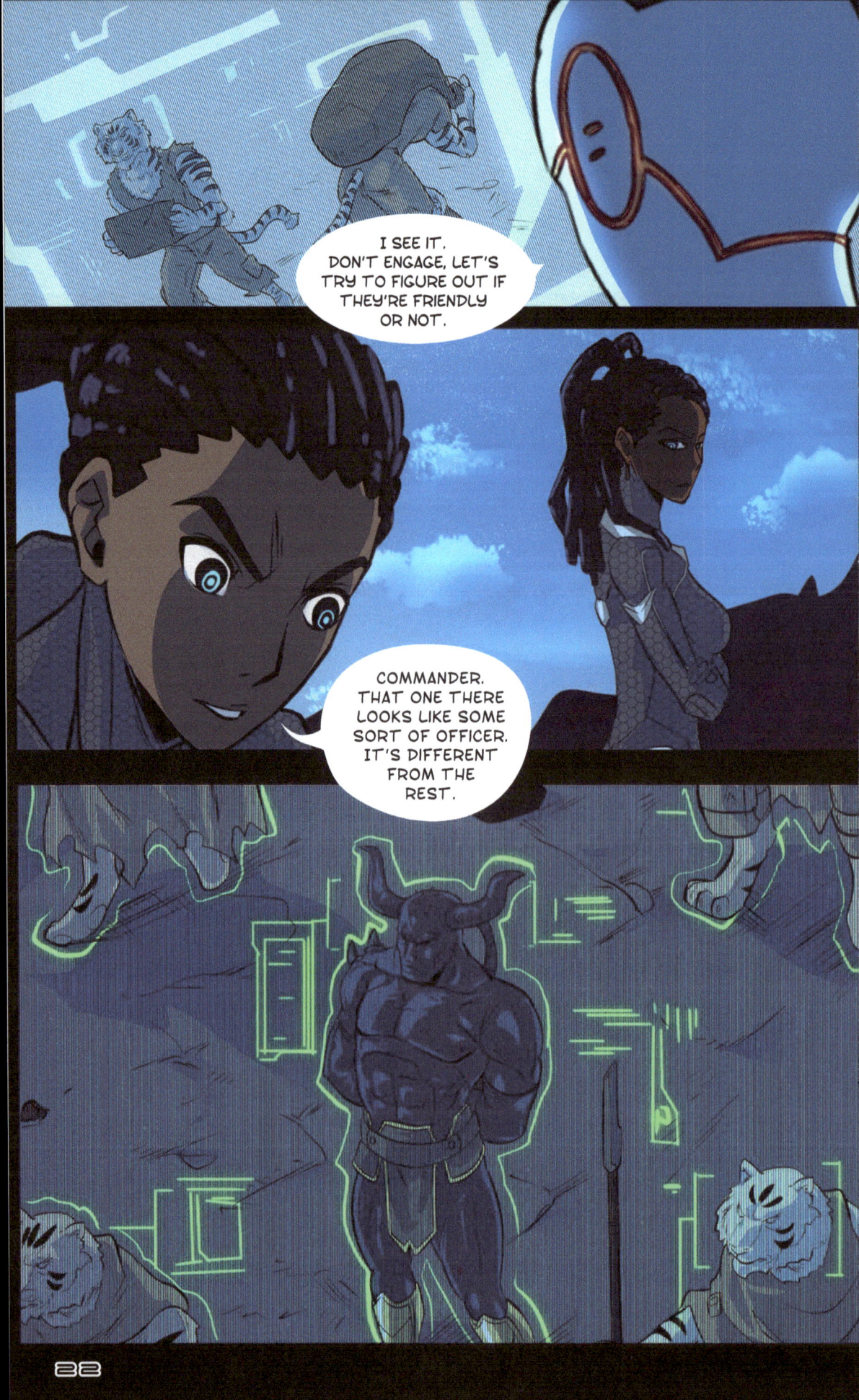

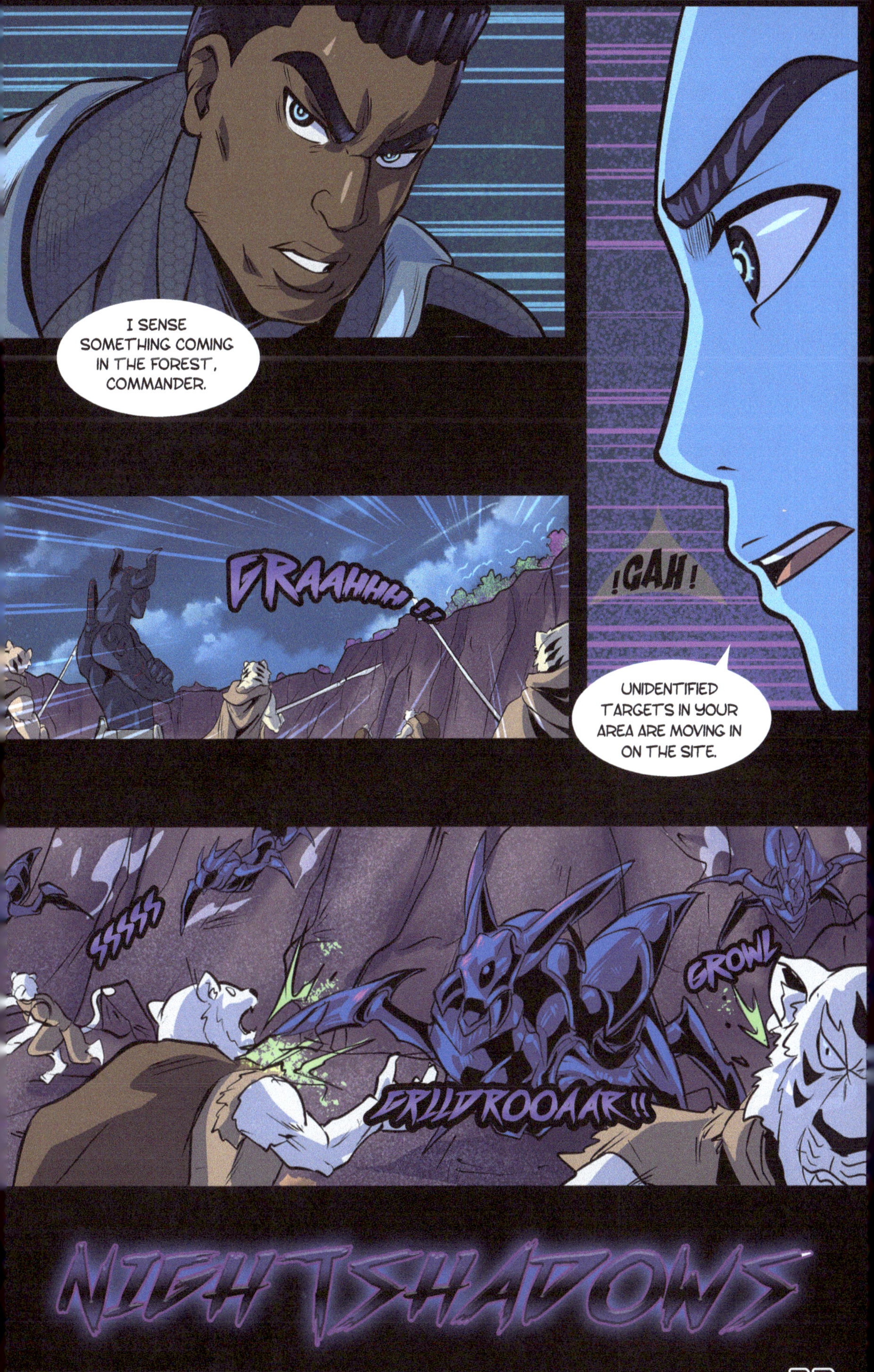

SENS!'IL STUDIOS

READ TODAY

OFFICIAL WEBSITE